"Marvelous"

It Happened in Riverdale, Volume 6

Juliana Harvard

Published by Juliana Harvard, 2021.

"MARVELOUS"

First edition. June 14, 2021.

ISBN: 979-8201765255

Written by Juliana Harvard.

Table of Contents

To Bill Johnson in a parallel universe

Chapter 1. Julie Goes to Beach City

Something was wrong, dreadfully wrong; Julie could feel it in the very air. *Why hadn't Allen written?* Too busy, of course, he would say. And it was true. With Allen working every spare moment at San Margo Academy, it was hard for him to keep up correspondence with parents, a brother, and a sweetheart a hundred miles away. But he had found time before. *Those rumors of those other girls—were they true? And what if they were? Must that be the end of Allen and Julie's love? Was she still in love? Why did she feel this creeping, cold complacency?*

"Don't you hope he's there!" an excited voice intruded.

"Huh?" Julie looked around. "Oh, I guess."

"Well, come on," urged her best friend Sandra, "let's get back to the building; it's almost time for supper."

Julie was fully aware of her surroundings now. Earlier that afternoon, the young people and the minister's wife, Mrs. Macintosh, had arrived at Beach City for the Youth Congress of the southwestern states. Julie, Sandra, and Allen's brother Peter had walked along the beach for a while. Now they saw the huge Sports Arena and adjacent municipal auditorium where the Youth Congress organizers held the meetings and served the meals.

Sandra scanned the crowds for a glimpse of Bob, her husband-to-be in just three summers. Sandra could not understand why Julie was not as excited to see Allen. In fact, neither could Julie.

"Julie!" called her young sister-like friend Darlene, "take your meal ticket. Meet you guys after the meeting; I'll be with Sandy." And, as she dashed away, Julie unconsciously watched Darlene's ponytail bob through the crowd. At that instant, she realized a presence—very near.

"Hi, there, Julie." It was an old, soft, familiar voice at her ear.

"Allen!" she whispered ecstatically, not being able to help being just a little delighted. But with a pre-determination to play the cool sophisticate—just until she was sure of him—she followed with a brief, "Hello, how are you?"

During supper, everything seemed to be just perfect. Bob, who had come 600 miles from Pacific Christian College that day, had found Sandra; and now they were inseparable. But deep inside Allen was tense, terribly tense. *Peter hadn't* meant *to tell him about Bill Johnson, the tall, dark, handsome stranger from Garden Grove; but somehow it had slipped. Would Julie tell him? If not, was he to bring it up? Just how* did *she feel, anyway?*

Allen looked at her for a long moment. *My Julie! So delicately pretty in her own little way.* He knew he could never forget her—with her patience, her endurance, and her loyalty. Nothing but a diabolical instinct could have made him so thoughtless and mean. He had hurt her—dreadfully—and he knew he must never hurt her again.

"Julie. Julie?"

Julie started. "What?" *How many times had Allen said her name before she responded?*

"Julie," Allen said, "you aren't listening."

"I'm tired."

"Thinking of 'marvelous'?"

Marvelous! Julie felt her mouth starting to fly open, but her pride held it shut. *How had Allen found out that "marvelous" was Julie's pet name for Bill Johnson?*

"Marvelous?" she repeated.

The feigned innocence in Julie's eyes amused Allen. "Peter told me all about it," he said in quiet seriousness. "Haven't you found him here yet?"

"No," Julie said sharply. "No, I haven't seen Bill Johnson."

Suddenly Allen felt fear—he didn't know why. His Julie seemed like a cold, fragile porcelain doll he could no longer reach. Once he got out of the building that night, he conveniently slipped away from her, retreating into his own little world to stall for time until he-didn't-know-what-or-when.

But the next morning at breakfast, even though they talked, an invisible but thick cloud hung between Allen and Julie. And soon thereafter, he disappeared again with a nonchalant, "And I'll see *you* subsequently!"

A strange sense of freedom came over Julie. *Bill* has *to be here, some place.* Those girls from Garden Grove had said that the Garden Grove fellows were staying at the Lafayette Hotel. Perhaps after morning devotion...

"Which discussion group are you going to?" Peter asked when they had finished praying.

"How about the one on 'Sound and Communication'?" Julie suggested.

"Say, that sounds pretty good! Where is it?"

Julie looked at her program. "Supper Room, Lafayette Hotel."

The discussion group was excellent, but there was no sign of Bill. "Call for him at the desk, please, Peter?" But Bill was not there. Dejectedly, Julie walked back to the Sports Arena with Peter.

"What *is* wrong with Allen?" Sandra asked Julie. "This isn't right; we four should be together, like at Christmas. Doesn't he realize what he's doing?"

"I don't know," Julie said helplessly.

Bob shook his head. "That Allen! He's been cold to *us,* too. I can't figure him out."

"Confidentially, Julie, don't you still love him?" Sandra, who spoke so tenderly, was so much in love.

Julie stared straight ahead at nothing. "I don't know, Sandra. I just don't know. If he's only discouraged because he thinks I'm stuck on Bill," she tried to explain, "then all it'll take is a little lovin' to pep him up. But if he really doesn't love me—" Her voice choked. This wasn't right; something *had* to give—and soon.

Chapter 2. Julie and Allen Break Up

After the morning seminars, it was time for lunch. Then there was a concert, richly eloquent in its beauty, given by the participating choirs and orchestras. Julie was content to be with Darlene and her girlfriend Sandy. She had even almost forgotten to look for Bill any more. But down deep inside, cast away temporarily, Julie felt that growing emptiness. She should be with Allen, sharing all this—the prayers, the worship, the music—together.

"Julie! There they are!" Darlene was poking her again. Who *this* time? Julie looked.

"Mrs. Macintosh and Allen!" Julie strained her eyes to look across the huge auditorium. But she lost sight of them; and when she looked a moment later, they had disappeared.

"I want to find him," Julie said in a strange tone. "We've got some talking to do." She rose quickly and left, leaving the other girls a little bewildered.

"Where are you going?" Darlene called. But Julie did not hear.

For the next three hours, no one saw Julie or Allen. No one knew Julie had followed Allen down the stairs, through the lobby, and up the escalator until she had cornered him in an alcove off the top balcony where no one sat. No one saw Allen and Julie make their way down from the balcony, cross the lobby, and start down the stairs that led to the banquet room. At the foot of the stairway was a cool, dimly lit niche. There was a square pond where three small palm trees grew. Several white stone benches surrounded it. Everything seemed like a well-written drama.

Julie finally put into words the question that had first prompted her to leave the concert. "Allen, do you still love me?"

"Yes," he replied slowly and deliberately. "But it's a different kind of love, Julie." *Not the kind of love one marries for,* she could hear Bob saying.

Allen went on. "Not the sickening sentimental kind of love that we used to believe would just last forever and ever."

Julie was crying now, her face buried deep in Darlene's sweater she had borrowed.

It was not the first time he had seen her cry, but a new sense of responsibility grasped Allen. He put his arm around the sobbing girl, but neither of them spoke.

Julie's sobs came in spurts. At first, she only shook her head and buried her face. She could not speak.

Allen's voice was not unkind. "A teenager has many loves," he said. "It's normal, Julie." *Is it, Allen?* she wanted to scream at him. *Why would it be normal to let go of genuine love once you've found it?*

She asked pensively, "Do you think we were *ever* really in love?"

"Yes, I do," was Allen's quiet reply. "And we wanted to believe it would never end. But we were so very young—only sixteen." Now Allen lifted her chin and forced her eyes to meet his. "Smile," he said lightly.

Bill Johnson is seventeen, Julie thought. *Maybe Bill is not too young to know genuine love...*

She relaxed and giggled slightly. "I'm curious," she said. "Just how long have you felt this way?"

Allen smiled. "Oh, since about the first of February, I guess. A couple months." *Since I first went out with Mindi,* he thought.

She nodded. "That's what I thought."

"How did you know?" A peculiar smile played on his face.

"Oh, a girl can sense it. The conveniently forgotten valentine in the rush of helping plan for the February 14 banquet you took Mindi to!"

Allen smiled sheepishly. "You're going to like being free," Allen said. "It's, well, it's—"

"I know," Julie said almost impishly. *In my mind, Allen, I broke up with you quite a while ago. I have been free. I've known how it feels for quite a while. I don't feel guilty anymore about Bill or anyone.*

Allen spoke again. "There's 'marvelous'—"

Julie laughed. "Oh, honestly, Allen! I only saw him that one night when Kurt and Peter and Sandra and I went to Garden Grove. I hardly even know him—" But she stopped. *Why was she making excuses now?*

"But he's moving to Riverdale this summer, Peter told me."

"Um-hum." She smiled sweetly. "Maybe you can meet him when you're home from San Margo Academy."

"Let's go back now," he said, putting his hand on her shoulder. "It's getting late. Hey, I think it's almost time for supper."

Chapter 3. Julie and Bill on Rainbow Pier

"Would you like to sit with us, Bob and Sandra and me, during the last meeting?" Julie asked Allen as they were eating supper.

Allen nodded. "Let's meet just inside the main door of the Sports Arena at, say, a quarter to seven," he suggested. Then they went their separate ways.

Finding Bob and Sandra, Julie smiled sweetly. Sandra, holding on to Bob's arm, looked around. "Julie!" she cried. "Where's Allen?" There was a definite tone of disappointment in Sandra's voice, and tears welled in the corners of her eyes.

"No, Sandra!" Julie protested. "No 'triste' now. It's all over." Julie could not allow her best friend to feel a sadness that she could no longer give in to.

Bob looked at his "little sis" with a tender understanding. "Just how did it happen, Julie?"

Julie smiled. She knew Bob and Sandra wanted to know out of their concern for her.

"Let's go sit down some place," Bob continued, "and you can tell us the entire story." And so they did until a quarter of seven.

The three of them were waiting for Allen by the main door when Sandra excused herself. "Be right back," she said. "I'm thirsty."

A minute later Allen appeared. Then he, Julie, and Bob were waiting for Sandra when suddenly she burst through the doorway with a tall, dark, handsome stranger. Not seeing Allen at first, she exclaimed, "Julie, Julie! I was just walking around out there and look who I found!"

Julie looked and instinctively stretched out her arms. "Bill!" she cried excitedly.

"Hi, there!" Bill said, accepting her embrace. His voice was soft but just as excited.

"Bill," she said, trying desperately to calm down, "there's someone I'd like you to meet." She turned to see Allen talking to a friend from San Margo and pretending to be unaware of what had just taken place. "Excuse me, Allen," she said sweetly, "I'd like you to meet Bill Johnson. Bill, Allen Macintosh."

As they shook hands and exchanged greetings, a strange feeling of pride swelled in Julie. Presently Allen said, "Well, I guess I'd better go now."

"Oh, you don't have to go now," Julie said. "We'll all sit together."

Julie, please stop being facetious—or naïve, Allen's eyes said, and he shook his head. "I'll see you later." And he watched Julie walk away with Bill.

The meeting was exceptionally good. Julie and Bill, with Sandra and Bob, enjoyed it. Although they had only seen each other once before in their lives—and Bill had even forgotten her name—they felt like old friends as they sat and talked and teased each other.

"Don't you *really* remember my name?" she asked.

"No," he laughed. "Please tell me."

"I don't think I will," she teased. "Just make up a name you think fits me."

He thought a minute. "How about 'Kitten'?" So Kitten Julie was ever after that.

After the meeting that night, Sandra and Bob introduced Bill to Mrs. Macintosh and Darlene and the rest of the little Riverdale group when they met at their appointed post.

"Let's go for a walk," Sandra suggested eagerly. "It's such a pretty night—the stars and the sea..." Her voice faded as she looked toward

Mrs. Macintosh for approval. The rest of the kids—except for Allen—joined Sandra's plea.

And so it was that a little group of couples and a few adult chaperones and some younger kids—minus Allen who waited in the car—strolled around Rainbow Pier. Julie's hand was safely tucked into Bill's. His hands were large and soft and seemed to hold her hand with a confident tenacity, as if he wanted to never let her go. As she looked up into his laughing blue eyes, she felt a magic there that she had to admit she had never felt with Allen. *What does this all mean?*

For a lovely hour they were together before they said their good nights. Bob left first, kissing his sweetheart and "sister," but knowing he and Sandra would be together in just five months at Pacific Christian College.

Bill found his mother, Lena, and introduced her to Mrs. Macintosh. Then he said good night to Julie, not knowing just when he would see her again. He only knew he would write.

"Good night, Kitten," he said, looking down at her affectionately. "I had a marvelous time tonight."

"So did I!" she smiled. "I hope I'll see you again in Riverdale."

He grinned and winked. "You can count on it!"

The next morning, everyone busily packed to go back to Riverdale. Since Julie had come with Macintoshes, she rode back with them in their car. She thought a great deal about Bill Johnson, however, remembering their romantic moonlight walk together on Rainbow Pier the night before. He was *so* cute! Tall, dark, and handsome, with a dimpled smile and a soft voice that made her melt. *Could he possibly ever like her as much as she liked him?*

Chapter 4. Julie's Ride Home from Beach City

Allen drove part of the way back home to Riverdale. But because of his fatigue, Mrs. Macintosh took over. Allen climbed into the back seat beside Julie.

"Hi, there," he began, and immediately took her hand. Julie tensed. *What was going to happen? Did Allen mean it—was he sorry for what had happened yesterday? Or was he only trying to prove to himself and to everyone else in the car that Julie was "easy to get"?* Julie slipped her hand out of his.

"Please hold hands with me."

"Why should I?" Both Allen and Julie were very facetious now.

"Because you want to."

"You're sitting beside me. That's enough."

"Whole hog or none."

Julie sighed inwardly as her apprehension grew. *This sounded and acted like the old Allen. Was there to be another horrible ten months—or more?* Every minute of the way home Julie was conscious of his every move. If he was sincere, she didn't want to hurt him. But she would *not let* Allen play her for a fool.

Allen helped her with carrying her things to her door. But his stiff expression as he muttered, "Goodbye, Stuck-up," left Julie with a very uncomfortable feeling.

It did not surprise Julie when she answered the phone that night to find Allen on the other end.

"Hi, how are you?" he greeted as usual.

"Fine. And you?"

"Okay." There was a brief pause. "Julie, I—I just called to say, well, I'm sorry...for the way I acted tonight. I don't mean to hurt you, honest, Julie. I—I guess I just acted without thinking."

"Don't we all?" she replied softly.

"Oh, I know," he said. "But I acted so selfishly. I *am* sorry, Julie. Please forgive me."

Julie hardly knew what to say. Many, many times in the past she had heard the same apologetic plea and listened to promises that Allen had broken. But somehow she believed Allen meant it this time. He was not emotional, but his voice was filled with warmth.

"Okay," she finally whispered. Then, "Are you coming to the youth prayer meeting tonight?"

"No, I've got *so* much homework. See you...sometime. 'Bye."

"'Bye." And her heart echoed, "Goodbye, dear Allen—goodbye."

Allen continued to date Mindi back at San Margo Academy. He came home to Riverdale once after Youth Congress. He and Peter enjoyed the company of Sandra and Kurt and Julie, as always. Meanwhile, Julie received letters from Bill and saw much more of him on the weekends when he and his mother Lena came to Riverdale to look for a house. But after that magic April day in Beach City, Allen and Julie's relationship remained the same. While she graciously accepted his apologies for his crummy behavior, she no longer gave in to his pleas for "another chance" to love her in the same way as before.

Chapter 5. After Julie's Graduation

Soon Julie's life was filled with the excitement of graduation from Highview Academy. It didn't matter anymore that Allen wasn't around to share it with her. She had just been awarded a California State Scholarship and could go to college next fall. And Bill and his mother Lena were going to move to Riverdale just as soon as school was out.

Sandra had just spent her freshman year at La Paloma College, only 35 miles away from Riverdale. But this summer she was working at *Snackies* as she was planning to go up north to Pacific Christian College to be with Bob in the fall. She had also talked Julie into going with her and being her roommate. It was going to be so much fun! But then Julie's Momma had changed her mind about letting her go so far away from home.

Now the summer was almost over. Then in sauntered Julie.

Sandra brought ice water to the short brunette who had already seated herself on a snack bar stool. "You're our best customer—for water, that is! Been shopping?"

"Oh, I just picked up my bedspread and rug at Woolworth's, since *our* plans for rooming together fell through."

"Oh, Julie, don't you think there's *any* more hope? We've planned this for so long!"

"None." Julie shook her head. "Well, at least we've managed so far to get to be at Emorys' house every weekend for the Riverdale Youth Club socials. And *we* can't complain about that!"

Sandra's eyes sparkled. "Boy, we've sure had some great times on Saturday nights—and afternoons, too—haven't we?"

Julie nodded. "It's been a marvelous summer." She stared into the empty glass. Julie thought especially of the times when they had driven up to the Riverdale Bowl where the historical Riverdale Pageant was held every spring. During the past year, they had often gone up there on lazy Saturday afternoons. They had found a secret entrance into the back of the outdoor stage set, complete with two large hay pits which the actors jumped into during scenes when they were supposed to be falling off the adobe roofs.

The very first time Julie and Bill and Sandra and Bob went to the hay pits was when Bob had come down from college after spring quarter. After discovering what fun it was to jump into the hay pits and "accidentally" fall on top of each other, Bob and Sandra eventually got tired and found that snuggling together in the hay came naturally.

Afterward they gathered on the flat rock at the base of the live oak tree whose dark green branches were silhouetted in the pale hazy sky. Far across the parched field the jagged purple mountains rose, hiding the softly fading gold and crimson that streaked the June sky. Not even a breeze was astir as the most welcome coolness settled over the warm earth. Julie gazed into the sunset, keenly aware of Bill's presence and his arm around her shoulder.

After their quiet evening worship prayer of thankfulness, it was a long moment before anyone could speak. Then magically their voices united in a simple hymn as the stars appeared like little lights in the window of heaven.

Even after Bob had gone back to Pacific Christian College for the rest of the summer, Julie and Bill and Kurt and Sandra had continued to sneak into the Riverdale Bowl and "play" in the hay pits on Saturday afternoons. Sometimes Darlene or Peter Macintosh would be with the group, too. And, with Kurt and Bill around, Sandra and Julie hadn't spent one Saturday night at home since that magic weekend last April at Beach City.

Now Julie's gaze shifted to Sandra. "What about Bob?"

Vivacious Sandra grew even more restless. "Oh, Julie, I don't know! I can't wait to get up north at Pacific Christian College with Bob—before it's too late."

"Too late for what?" Julie handed her the empty water glass.

"Julie—I'm falling in love with Kurt. I actually *want* to let him kiss me. And it's not right! It's not fair to Bob—he's waited so long."

"Kurt!" Julie was stunned. "I know the four of us have been together all summer, especially at Riverdale Bowl. Wasn't it neat that just last Saturday night Bill asked me to go steady? But you and Kurt—"

"Oh, I know. Kurt has liked me secretly for a long time. He was so afraid that when you and Bill had that big quarrel after your graduation that the four of us would never be together again."

Julie winced as she remembered. "I know, that was so stupid. You know, I almost lost Bill for good! He was so sure that I still loved Allen. It was all I could do to convince him that everything is over with Allen."

"Oh, Julie, Bill belongs with you. But Kurt is so sweet and gentle...." Sandra shook herself. "What am I saying? I belong with Bob!"

Julie smiled. "As if you should worry. I have to tell you this, but *please*, don't tell Bill. Promise?"

Sandra leaned forward eagerly. "Yes? Tell me!"

"Well, Allen wants to date me again—I don't know why. After the suddenness of that episode at Beach City when he left me for blonde, beautiful Mindi, it's hard to believe he wants me back. Especially how I carried on with the 'marvelous' Bill Johnson that same Saturday night!"

"Julie!" Sandra spoke with playful sternness. "You know good and well—no matter what happened in the past—Allen is in love with you. Always has been, always will be—and is *now!*"

Julie shook her head adamantly. "Doesn't matter. I'm Bill's girl now."

Sandra fetched a glass for herself. "Say, aren't you rather looking forward to staying here in Riverdale Valley this fall? Especially now that Bill and Lena Johnson have moved to Riverdale..."

"But I won't see him except for when I come home on leave. And you know that freshmen only get to come home every six weeks." Julie sighed. "I'm really glad that Allen will be almost a hundred miles from La Paloma after school starts when he goes back to San Margo Academy for his senior year."

"I bet Allen will try to find some way to get to La Paloma to visit you, don't you think?"

Julie only sighed, shaking her head, trying to change the subject. "Sandra, I wanted to go to Pacific Christian College as badly as you do!"

Silently, Sandra set down her glass then leaned on the counter, her chin in her hands and her eyes fastened on Julie. "Oh, really, now?!"

Julie stood up. "W-well, *almost* as badly as you do. See you!"

Sandra laughed as Julie's well-rounded figure slipped out the door and into her car. She returned the bewitching grin before Julie put on her glasses and drove away. Then the long shining black hair behind the steering wheel disappeared as Julie's Rambler got lost in traffic.

Chapter 6. Julie Goes to College

The weeks passed quickly, bringing the late-summer heat wave then the falling leaves. And it put 600 miles between two girls who had been best friends since fifth grade.

"...and I had only been on campus ten days before a boy asked me for a date! Glen is a pre-med and wanted me to spend a weekend in the mountains at his parents' cabin! But Bill surprised me on Saturday afternoon by driving up to the college, since I couldn't go off campus yet. I even forgot to call Glen back to tell him no..." Sandra chuckled out loud.

"What is it, roommate?"

"Oh, Anna, it's just a letter from my friend at home, Julie Scott. It's only October, but it sounds like she's really having a ball. No," she muttered half to herself, "I don't need to worry about her. I just hope things will work out for Bob and me."

"...but the very night Glen disappeared, Larry asked me to the Wednesday night concert on campus. Man, Bill was really jealous when I told him, but I assured him that Larry is just a friend..."

"...I thought Allen's phone call from San Margo was really something. Then when he sent the flowers for my birthday, I could hardly believe it. Sandra, do you think maybe he really does still like me? Well, it's way too late for him. He had his chance!"

Sandra hesitated to pick up the pen. Slowly she wrote, "Dear Julie, I guess you're having a great time down there, aren't you? Oh, I'm so mixed up I don't know what to do! Bob wants to get married next summer, and I'm not even sure I'm in love with him. No, it's not Kurt—I just don't know. We've had some great times together—he does everything he can for me—I *just don't have the feelings I should have. I want to love him, really I do, but I hardly know him—we've been apart so long. And what should I take for my major? Daddy's always plugged for the teacher idea, but I want to be a social worker—or maybe even Bob's wife..."*

And Julie wrote back, this time surprising even Sandra. *"Sandra, I really have to tell you this. I just can't wait until I see you at Christmas time. Bill Johnson is absolutely the most wonderful man in the world! He was so patient with me when Glen and Larry were trying to date me, and even when he knew Allen sent me the flowers for my birthday in October. I can't wait to see you and tell you in person about what happened during Thanksgiving vacation when I went home to Riverdale. You know, Lena Johnson is becoming like a second mother to me.... Things will work out for you and Bob. He's loved you deeply for over two years—even when he was supposedly dating me. Anyway, your decision about a major will come, too; magically, someday you'll know exactly what you want..."*

Chapter 7. Christmas Vacation in Riverdale

The Christmas spirit permeated the air the day Sandra packed and said goodbye to Bob. "I sure wish you were going back to Riverdale with me, honey."

"Well, princess, I do, too. But, well, we need the money. We both have debts to pay off. Now you be good while you're home! And, merry Christmas, sweetheart!"

Sandra returned his kiss and got onto the plane. As the silver machine soared through the clouds, she knew this vacation would be the real test of her love for Bob—when she would be around Kurt once more.

"Oh, Julie, long time no see!" Sandra spoke into the telephone. "Let's get together and have a nice long talk—you must tell me all about you and Bill— Wait a minute! Daddy just brought the car home—I'll be right over!"

Sandra found one gay girl sitting by the tree and an admiring Bill looking on as she opened his gift. Unnoticed, Sandra stood by the door as Bill and Julie shared a sweet Christmas kiss. There was no need to even ask about Allen anymore!

"Sandra! Come on in," called Julie. "Hey, how about tonight?"

"Kurt would sure like to see you," Bill winked.

"We-l-l—" Sandra blushed slightly.

"Come on, I'll call him and tell him you're here." Julie rose to her feet and grabbed the phone. Sandra started to protest—but didn't.

Soon Kurt and Sandra and Bill and Julie were on their way to the church to pick up a couple of carol books. But their caroling trip got no farther. By the time they had agreed on what carols to use, what parts each would sing, and so on, the hands of the chapel clock had almost reached ten.

"So long!" Bill called as Kurt pulled out from Julie's driveway. Then he turned to Julie.

"Well, sweetheart, I'll see you New Year's Eve." Bill kissed her lips gently.

"A-hem!" Sandra teasingly cleared her throat loudly.

Julie sighed softly as Bill's car, too, disappeared into the darkness. "Have fun tonight, Sandra?"

"Huh?" Sandra started from her daydreaming. "Oh, yeah, I guess so. I, uh, see you and Bill are, uh—"

"Oh, Sandra," Julie drooled, "it's really neat now! Nothing will *ever* keep Bill and me apart again!"

Sandra beamed. "I know. I'm really in love with Bob. Last summer—" She laughed and shook her head. "Kurt is just a boy. It was just a summer fling. You know, Julie, tonight was really boring with Kurt. I mean, I *like* Kurt; but I *love* Bob. I'm sure of it now."

"I'm happy for you," Julie reflected, "almost as happy as I am with Bill!" Julie remembered Sandra's many past dilemmas with romance. Every fellow had literally swept Sandra off her feet, but somehow never seemed to quite fill the place in Sandra's heart. This time, Julie was sure Bob would fill that place.

"Mrs. Julie Johnson," Sandra teased. "Well, I'll see you spring vacation—if I can tear myself away from Bob for five days!"

"Okay, Mrs. Sandra Miller," Julie returned. "Be sure to write!"

Julie and Sandra waved goodbye as long as they could see each other. Then, once again, the two girls went their separate ways.

After Christmas, Julie could come home from La Paloma College much more often. Bill had already become the most popular senior boy at Riverdale High, and all the girls were dying to date him. They couldn't understand how he could go steady with a girl he didn't see every day. But Bill had grown very fond of Julie and knew that she had something very special. Someday he would find out just how special she would be to him.

Chapter 8. Bill's Senior Prom

The weeks passed quickly, and it would soon be time for Bill's graduation. Unlike the year before, when Julie had graduated, and Julie and Bill had almost split up afterwards, this year Julie and Bill knew each other so much better. After spring vacation, just one year after their romantic walk on Rainbow Pier in Beach City, they had seen each other nearly every weekend, even if it had to be a quick trip home for Julie on just Saturday night.

Julie and Bill spent every moment together when Julie was home from college. Sandra and Bob were away at Pacific Christian College, and Kurt and Peter and Darlene seemed to always be busy doing other things. Bill was really glad that Allen Macintosh was away at San Margo Academy. Julie never even mentioned his name any more.

Of course, the highlight of Bill's senior year was taking Julie to his senior prom. Now he could really show her off! He stood more than a foot above her in height, his 6'4" frame towering over her petite 5'2" frame. She looked so pretty in her baby pink ballerina-length spaghetti-strap prom dress, Bill thought. And they danced well together, despite their difference in height.

It was after midnight when a tired but happy couple climbed into Bill's old '57 Chevy and drove out of the Riverdale High parking lot. But Bill did not head toward Julie's house.

"Where are we going?" she asked him.

Bill grinned. "You'll see," was all he would say.

Julie looked around and soon recognized that they were on their way up to Riverdale Bowl. They had never gone there at night before! "Bill?" Julie questioned. But then she was silent, wondering and waiting.

Instead of stopping at the edge of the now-deserted asphalt parking lot, Bill turned into an obscure dirt road, just wide enough for his Chevy. Julie chuckled.

"I didn't know this road was here!" she said.

"Neither did I," Bill said, "until last week when I was just driving around up here. It goes almost up to the hay pits. Must be how the Riverdale Pageant cast gets up here when the shows are going on."

Bill turned off the headlights just before pulling the car to a gentle stop. Julie looked around at the distant barren hills and the yellow moon that had risen from behind the hazy purple mountains, now cloaked in misty darkness. Neither of them spoke for a long moment. Julie felt Bill's arm slip around her shoulder.

"Baby," he whispered, very close to her ear, "tonight was so very special. Thank you for going to the senior prom with me. I'm so glad you're my girl!"

Julie sighed contentedly as she leaned her head onto his broad, soft shoulder. "So am I!" she breathed, wiggling just a little to be even closer to him.

Now his warm lips nuzzled her ear, and she giggled slightly. "I love you, Julie," he whispered, kissing her neck. She felt a tingle and moaned softly. Then she turned her face toward his.

"Oh, Bill! I never thought I'd ever find a boy like you. And," she hesitated, "I wasn't sure you'd ever really like me, anyway. I mean, Sandra is so much cuter. And Kurt and Bob are both in love with her—"

Bill put his finger on her lips. "Shh!" he remonstrated. "I don't want to hear it. All I want is you." And he kissed her tenderly.

Julie squirmed as she put her hands on Bill's neck and pulled closer to him as they kissed. She felt his lips part and then felt his warm, wet tongue tracing the outline of her lips. Her own tongue was quick to meet his. Now Bill, too, let out a soft moaning sound.

On such a warm May night, Bill soon needed to roll down the car windows. Julie jumped just a little and looked around. "Don't worry," he laughed. "No one ever comes up here." He looked back at Julie, his eyes searching hers as if for an answer to some unspoken question. She returned his gaze for a long moment, half-frightened, half-fascinated with what she was feeling at this moment. *Did Bill feel it, too?*

"I love you, baby," Bill repeated, as he leaned in again to kiss her. Her lips parted readily now, and her breathing quickened. Bill moved his hand to her shoulder and gently slipped one spaghetti strap of her prom dress down, caressing her bare arm. She shivered suddenly, as she felt his large soft hand cupping her breast lightly and then continuing to caress her as they kissed. Bill's face was warm, and his breathing, too, had sped up.

"Do you love me as much as I love you?" he whispered now, his voice strange with a new tenseness that Julie had never heard before.

"Oh, yes, Bill, I *do* love you!" Even her own voice sounded unfamiliar to her now, more intense, more passionate than she could ever have imagined before now.

Bill took Julie's hand into his and caressed it with his other hand. He drew her fingers up to his lips and kissed them, wordlessly, and then sucked gently on her pretty index finger with the Pink Pearl nail polish she had chosen just to match her prom dress. She watched him, enthralled, unable to speak.

Bill and Julie kissed again, but this time he held her hand in his as he dropped it into his lap. She was half-startled, half-embarrassed to feel the hard bulge inside his pants, and instinctively pulled her hand away quickly. But he placed his hand on top of hers. "Your hand feels so good there," he whispered into her ear, this time running his tongue around the outer edge of her left ear.

She relaxed and let her hand fall naturally around the place where Bill had put it. Curious, she squeezed just a little and then felt Bill's entire body suddenly stiffen and heard a quick gasp from his lips. Their deep kiss grew even more intense, though she wasn't sure how it could get any more passionate.

Chapter 9. Going All the Way

Suddenly Bill pulled away, clearing his throat, and opened his car door. Of course the inside light came on, and he reached up quickly to switch it off.

"What's wrong?" Julie asked, a little confused.

"Nothing," Bill said, "nothing at all, my dear." He stood up outside on the grassy meadow and held out one hand toward her. "Come here, Sugar."

Julie slid across the seat and under the steering wheel as he guided her gently toward him. Then they stood together, embracing, and he kissed her forehead. "Isn't it beautiful up here at night?" It was more of a statement than a question.

"What are we doing here?" she ventured, noticing that they were very near the hay pits behind the stage house.

He took her hand, and they walked several steps. Now she could see they were only a few yards from the all-too-familiar hay pits.

"Remember last summer," he began, "and the first time we ever kissed?"

Julie smiled, remembering it well. "Yeah, we first kissed down there, huh?" She pointed to the nearby hay pit.

He gave her an extra squeeze now. "Come on," he urged, pulling at her slightly, "just for old times' sake."

"Bill!" she protested. "Look at me. I can't go down there in my high heels!"

"Then I'll carry you," he replied quickly, grinning. And before she knew what was happening, Bill had swept her up, lifting her easily into his arms, prom dress and all, as she clung tightly to his neck, laughing. But, without a word, he turned and headed back to the car. Julie had stopped fighting him, and leaned her head against his, feeling that one stray lock of his soft brown hair falling onto her cheek.

When they got back to his car, he put her down gracefully, his arm still encircling her tiny waist. But it was the back car door that he opened. He sat down inside the car and reached out for her now with both hands. For a dizzying moment she hesitated.

"I love you, Kitten." Bill's voice was warm and almost pleading. *How could she resist him now? How could she resist the warm feelings within her own heart?*

She took his hands and let him pull her into the car. "Oh, Bill," she breathed, "you are just so... so marvelous!"

They began kissing again, more fervently than before, as Bill leaned back onto the car seat and pulled Julie down on top of him. He ran his fingers through her long, silky, dark hair and across her bare shoulders. As she lay on top of him, she could still feel the large lump in his pants, now pressing hard against her lower tummy, even through the layers of crinoline underneath her dress. She felt something akin to electricity seeming to start between her legs and surge outward through her entire body. She felt her hips moving in a slow rhythm against his....

It was not quite daylight when Julie awoke, startled for only a moment to find Bill's still-sleeping body mostly on top of her. Fully awake, she remembered clearly what had just happened a few hours before. She stirred, and Bill opened his eyes, smiling at her.

"Good morning, baby," he said tenderly. "I love you, Kitten."

"Bill!" she whispered, taking a deep breath. "What have we just done?"

He kissed her slightly trembling lips. "I love you, Kitten," he repeated.

Julie sat up now. She was wearing blue jeans and a sweater. She had crumpled the prom dress in the front seat. Ah, yes! She had had the extra clothes in her overnight bag because Bill was going to take her directly back to La Paloma after the prom even though she had signed out of the dorm to be at her home in Riverdale until Sunday. But the way things had turned out—well, at least she had gotten dressed afterwards. And no one had discovered them in Bill's car!

"Momma thinks I went back to the college last night," she said, more to herself than to Bill. "What if she calls?"

"She won't call before six a.m.," Bill said coolly. "We've got plenty of time to get there." He sat up beside her.

Julie dropped her head onto Bill's chest and sighed. After a few moments she said, "We need to go."

Wordlessly, she crammed her dress into her overnight bag and climbed over into the front seat. Bill got out of the car, adjusted his clothing slightly, and settled in under the steering wheel.

They spent most of the ride from Riverdale back to La Paloma in silence. The sun was just beginning to come up, tinting the sky with a brilliant yellow-orange on a silent early Sunday morning. Once they were out onto the highway, Bill dropped his right hand down onto the seat over Julie's hand. She returned his gentle squeeze.

Julie knew that the back gate of the chain lock fence surrounding the girls' side of campus would be unlocked by 6 a.m., and that Bill's turquoise '57 Chevy could drive up unnoticed and let her out very close to the back basement door of the girls' dorm. Although neither had ever done anything like this before, they were quite familiar with many stories of other daring students who had done similar things.

At long last, Bill spoke. "You have finals the week before my graduation, don't you?" He already knew that, but said it anyway.

Julie nodded. "I'll be home then, at least for three weeks before summer school starts."

Again, silence froze their words as the brick dormitory rose into plain sight. Bill stopped the car just inside the gate. He looked at Julie for a long moment, wanting to say something, but he didn't know what.

"Are you...okay?" he said, at last.

A broad smile spread across Julie's face now. "Yes," she said, giggling. "Marvelous!" And she disappeared into the back door of the dorm.

Chapter 10. Bill's Summer Job

Graduation Day 1964 brought a great deal of celebration and festivity to Riverdale. By this time, though, Bill and Kurt had each found his own separate way and didn't pal around together much anymore. No one thought too much about it, but later Julie would find out some things that none of the other kids knew. Anyway, Kurt was going back east to some prestigious college. Bob and Sandra were coming home to Riverdale for the summer and would transfer from Pacific Christian College to La Paloma College in the fall. At long last, Sandra and Julie would get to be roommates.

Bill and Julie skipped the all-night graduation party at Riverdale High and spent the time alone together, since Julie would spend the summer on campus at La Paloma working for the summer-long National Science Institutes and taking classes, too. Bill would work in Riverdale for a local house painter, Mr. Lear.

"I don't like being away from you this summer," Julie told Bill as they sat in the porch swing at his house.

"You know how hard I tried to get a job on campus at La Paloma," he reminded her, "but there just isn't anything available for me until fall. Anyway, painting will pay a lot more."

Julie frowned, even as she hugged him. "I know," she admitted, "but Mr. Lear's daughter Beth is just too cute for you to be around!"

Bill laughed, surprised. "I don't love Beth, honey," he assured her. "I love you."

Several weeks later, when Julie came home for a weekend, she found out just how right she had been. It was Sandra who told her what a hard crush Beth Lear had on Bill. But Julie waited to see what Bill would say about it.

Bill had been unusually quiet at the Emorys' Saturday night swimming pool party. Julie just figured he was tired at first, but then she could see that something was really bothering him.

"What's wrong, Bill?" she asked gently. "Did you have a hard week of painting?"

He shrugged. "Yeah, sort of, I guess." He did not return Julie's steady gaze.

"There's more, isn't there?" she ventured. "Please, baby, you can tell me."

"Well," he began, "I know you knew Beth had a crush on me from the beginning." He paused.

Julie nodded, but did not speak.

"She even came right out and asked me if I would be her boyfriend since you were away at college."

A shiver of fear shot through Julie, not totally sure of what Bill might say next. She waited for him to speak again.

Bill put his arm around Julie and squeezed her just a little, looking directly into her eyes. "Beth is pretty cute and all, but I'm not attracted to her." Julie breathed a secret sigh of relief as Bill went on.

"Last week Mr. Lear took me aside and told me in no uncertain terms that I was not good enough for his little girl, that I could never support her in the manner to which she was accustomed. It was a real slap in the face!"

For a brief instant Julie felt sympathy for Bill, but her feelings of relief were strong. She looked up into his tired eyes. "Oh, Bill, you know *my* Momma would never say something like that to you!"

Bill hugged her tightly. "I know, Sugar. You and I—well, we're just so right for each other. No one will ever take your place in my heart!"

Julie sighed, returning his embrace, settling into his arms for a very long time.

Chapter 11. Bill Almost Dies

The summer soon passed, though not quickly enough for Julie and Bill. When school started, he could get a job on the college farm, which meant that he had to get up very early hours. They tried to see each other as much as possible, but they had no classes together, and worked and ate at different times. It was only on the weekends they could spend much time together. But they cherished every precious moment together.

It wasn't long before Bill's 20 hours of work a week increased to 30 and sometimes 40. He was carrying a full class load and struggling just to stay awake in class, let alone keep his grades up.

"I wish you didn't have to work so much," Julie often said to him. "You're always so tired. You're going to get sick!"

Julie did not know then just how right her words would be. On the night before the beginning of Christmas vacation, Bill and Julie ate supper together in the college cafeteria. Then they went to the almost empty Student Center before Julie's drive home to Riverdale.

Bill put his arm on the back of the sofa and hugged Julie as closely as he dared, ready to move quickly if a faculty member walked in. Julie was sad and silent. "Oh, Bill," she said, "I wish you were coming home with me tonight!"

"So do I, baby," he whispered. "So do I! But you know I have to stay here and work during vacation. If I don't make enough money to pay my bill here, I won't be able to come back next semester."

Julie brushed away a tear, knowing how very much she would miss him. "I know," she choked. "I'm sorry."

"Hey," he smiled, "I'll be home on Christmas day. We'll be together then."

Julie nodded. "I can't wait," she whispered. Then, seeing that no one else was around for a moment, she leaned over until her lips met his.

Bill walked with Julie to her car and put her suitcase in the trunk. Once again he kissed her lightly and quickly before she got into the car. "We'll have real kisses on Christmas day!" he promised her.

But Christmas never came that year for Julie and Bill. It was the day before Christmas Eve that Julie called Bill's dorm to find out if he needed her to drive to La Paloma to get him. There seemed to be some confusion by the boys who answered the dorm phone. No one had seen Bill all day. Puzzled, she hung up and dialed Lena Johnson's number.

When Lena answered, she spoke quietly. Then she was silent for a very long time. "Julie," she said finally, "the assistant dean brought Bill home late last night."

A bolt of fear shot through Julie! *What was wrong? If anything ever happened to Bill, she just knew she would die!*

"He's very, very sick, honey," Lena breathed.

Julie began to cry. "Can I come over and see him, please, Lena?"

"Of course, dear," Lena answered. "For just a little while."

Julie walked into a quiet, tense house—a place where she had spent many happy hours with Bill and his mother Lena—now filled with impending doom. She was not prepared for what she saw, even though it had been not quite a week since she had last seen Bill.

He lay in his bed, still and pale, barely stirring as he opened his eyes briefly when Julie entered. He tried to reach his hand toward her, but it fell limply onto the bedcovers. He appeared gaunt, almost bony, and a chill followed by a hot flash of dread swept through her body. It startled her to hear a voice from the opposite side of the room.

"We've done all we can for now," the deep, eerie voice said.

"Dr. Gaston!" Julie exclaimed. "What are you doing here?"

The old man smiled thinly. "Some of us still *do* make house calls."

But you're a homeopathic, Julie wanted to wail at Kurt's father, *not a "real" doctor!* But Julie kept still. She looked at Lena and could tell that she had been crying. Now Julie's tears fell, too.

Julie sat carefully on the edge of Bill's bed and held his hand between hers. She felt the extremely high fever that now raged through Bill's very hot, limp hand. She bent down and gently kissed his cheek. "I love you, Bill," she whispered, stroking his unruly dark brown hair. "Please don't die, baby. Please don't die!"

The next few hours, or days, Julie didn't know which, were a bleak nightmare, something from a sad movie that doesn't seem like actual life. She remembered, in a blurry way, being at home for Christmas day, seeing her favorite cousin Sue, then going back to Bill's house, despite Momma's protest to "let that boy get well without you smotherin' him."

It was a sad and reluctant Julie who returned to La Paloma College after Christmas vacation. Bill was not really getting any better, despite Dr. Gaston's seeming to be at the Johnson house almost day and night. Julie had ignored him, staying close to Bill's side as much as possible, sleeping in a chair with her head on the side of Bill's bed and his hand placed limply on her neck. She would get up only when Lena came in periodically to see if Bill could drink water. But Bill could not eat or drink anything and could barely even breathe.

One night in desperation Lena had asked Bill if there was anything at all she could get for him.

"Vernor's Ginger Ale," he had replied weakly as he passed in and out of consciousness. Lena had come home with a six-pack.

But Bill could not swallow even one drop of his favorite soda. It foamed up on his mouth and ran down the side of his face. Julie was quick to wipe the foam from the side of Bill's face and allow him to spit the foam from his mouth. Bill continued to put small amounts into his mouth and the result was always the same, but it went in further each time. Finally, he could get it all the way into his mouth. The foam was a deep chocolate color when he spit it out. Much later, when Bill could talk, he told Julie that it had removed the "cotton dirt" feeling that he had in his mouth for weeks.

It was a full month later, however, when Bill's tonsils ruptured. When that happened, he could finally breathe normally again and slowly recovered. He had dropped to 87 pounds and had nearly died of malnutrition. He did not return to La Paloma College.

Julie focused hard on her studies that lonely second semester without Bill. She came home to Riverdale as often as possible and spent every minute that she could with Bill. He seemed sad and distant, quiet and pensive. But Julie didn't press him to talk. All she could do was love and hug him. Soon the summer would come, and this time Julie would be back home in Riverdale.

Chapter 12. Bill Gets Drafted

"You will be happy to know I will not be painting for Mr. Lear this summer," Bill announced to Julie on the first day she was home for the summer.

Julie grinned and hugged Bill tightly. "It's going to be so good to be here in Riverdale with you this summer," she cooed.

Bill was silent for a long moment, staring off into space. "I suppose I should tell you," he began.

Julie looked up at him, not quite knowing what to expect.

"I've got a full-time job at Knott's Berry Farm," he told her.

"Really!" Julie didn't know whether to laugh or cry. "But that's a long way to drive—"

Bill nodded. "I know, Sugar. It will mean early mornings and late nights—"

Julie grabbed him, almost shaking him. "Bill Johnson!" she cried. "That's what made you so sick last winter. You can't do this again!"

"It's different," he insisted. "Remember, I was also trying to carry a full load of classes then." He paused. "The pay is good, benefits are great, and—"

"And?" Julie thought she detected a hint of pain in his voice.

"And less time to have to spend in the house."

Now Julie was thoroughly baffled. She was speechless. *What is going wrong in Bill's family?*

Bill put his arms around Julie and hugged her tightly. "Sugar, let's go somewhere so we can talk."

Julie and Bill and his '57 Chevy made their way up the winding road to Riverdale Bowl. This time of year the stage house and the hay pits were deserted, and the late afternoon sun shone hot and bright on the barren fields. Julie, in her cut-off blue jean shorts and rubber flip-flops, held Bill's hand tightly as they made their way down to "their" hay pit. They settled into a partially shaded corner, Julie leaning back onto Bill in a very familiar way.

It had been over a year since their first night visit to Riverdale Bowl, the night of Bill's senior prom when they had stayed out all night and first made love. It was indeed "marvelous" as they continued to visit the hay pit alone as often as they could without risk of getting caught. They had also learned to use condoms, so there was no worry about getting Julie pregnant before they were ready.

Today, however, Bill had brought Julie up here for something totally different, a baring of his soul that stripped him far more naked than any baring of his body could. Today, as he turned Julie over on top of him, he hugged her closer than he ever had before. His hands trembled as he ran his fingers absentmindedly through her long silky dark hair.

Today Bill would tell Julie *exactly* what was going wrong, family secrets that no one but Julie—ever—would be privy to know. Today would be the first—but not the last—time that Julie would see Bill cry....

It was well past dark when Julie felt Bill stir under her, where they had both fallen into an exhausting sleep after their long ordeal. Julie felt the dried tearstains on her own cheeks, as she shared his tears, and she reached out in the darkness to touch Bill's face. She felt his arms tighten around her as she sensed fresh tears were flowing from Bill's eyes.

"Oh, Bill," she cried again, "I am *so* sorry! I wish there were something I could do!"

He touched her lips with his fingertips, her soft pink mouth he knew so well. "You *have* done something," he assured her. "You have listened to me, and you understand me, and you love me."

"More than anything or anyone else in the world," she whispered.

"And that's the most important thing that you can do, baby," he sighed. "I think I can make it through this—I don't know how, but I will—with you by my side."

"I'll always be here for you, Bill—for us," Julie said. "Forever and always, I promise!"

They kissed now, a long, sweet lip kiss that seemed to seal their hearts even closer together and bonded their very souls and spirits into one.

Julie understood now, more than she ever knew she could. She understood Bill could not return to La Paloma College that fall. She knew, too, the most likely consequence of a young man past age 18 who was not enrolled in school.

The summer passed too quickly, and once again Julie packed to move into the dormitory, once again rooming with Sandra Lee. Bill continued working and saw Julie on weekends as often as possible. Then came that fateful day in November when Bill received the letter that Julie had so much dreaded.

"Hi, baby!" Bill tried hard to sound cheerful on the phone, but Julie knew him so well that she could detect the slightest hint of something wrong.

"It happened, didn't it?" She got directly to the point.

Bill did not evade her question. "Yes, Sugar, I'm afraid I've been drafted into the United States Army."

Chapter 13. Julie Meets Howard

Julie was not sure how she was going to live without Bill for weeks and months at a time. She knew she *had* to come home to Riverdale the last weekend before Bill was to leave for Basic Training, even if it meant violating home leave regulations. She would just deal with any consequences when she came back to the dorm on Sunday night. For now, she had to be with Bill and spend one last "marvelous" night with him in the hay pit before the U.S. Army would ship him off to parts unknown.

Their lovemaking that night was unusually fervent and prolonged, each clinging to the other as if they could never let go. Being late fall, it was cooler than the summer nights they had spent here, and Bill had brought extra blankets. He was especially gentle with her, caressing her soft skin and snuggling close together, warming her body in ways that only he knew how to do.

It was not until she was back in the dorm on Sunday night, and Bill was well on his way to Fort Sam Houston, Texas, that Julie really broke down and sobbed. Sandra tried to comfort her.

Julie cried for what seemed like hours, then knew she had to pull herself together. She had to trust the love that she and Bill shared would carry them both through this. Two years seemed like such a long time! So much could happen.

In less than one year, Sandra and Bob would get married, right after their college graduation next June. So, between wedding plans and senior year activities and graduation plans, Sandra and Bob kept really busy.

Julie kept very busy writing letters to Bill and waiting for his occasional phone calls.

Their Christmas together—Bill's first home leave—was very special. It was much too cold now for a visit to the hay pit, but Bill's turquoise '57 Chevy was warm, and found its way to safe and private spots on obscure country roads. Of course, there was much more to talk about now as Bill shared his experiences as a soldier. Julie cherished every precious moment that they could spend together.

It was shortly after Christmas when Bill heard about Howard Davidson, a classmate of Julie's and fellow music major. Although Howard had transferred to La Paloma College the year before, Julie had never mentioned his name in her letters to Bill.

Howard Davidson was an exceptionally talented young organist and was in most of Julie's music classes. They had become instant friends, even last school year, enjoyed the same music, laughed at the same corny jokes from their professors. As keyboard students forced to take the same "other instrument" class, they had both squeaked through Dr. Walters' string instrument class together. Now Howard was finalizing plans to play the organ for Sandra and Bob's wedding this summer—in June 1966.

Even Sandra had noticed Julie's increasing time spent with Howard on campus. "Hey, what's with Howard, anyway?" she asked Julie.

"Oh, Sandra," Julie answered. "He is *such* a good friend! He's *so* smart—it really helps to study counterpoint with him."

"Hmm," Sandra queried, "are you sure that's *all* you're studying with him?"

Julie started to speak, then frowned. "Oh, kid, I don't know *what* it is! I know I love Bill dearly—enough to marry him if he ever asks me. But there's just something about Howard, something I can't explain, that draws us together. It's like a—a kindred spirit of sorts." She ended almost as if it were a question.

"Maybe it's that brother-sister thing," Sandra offered. "You know, like you and Bob, or you and Darlene."

But Julie shook her head. "I know that neither Howard nor I have siblings," she agreed, "but it's more than that. It's almost like—now don't take this wrong—like Howard is my best girlfriend!"

Sandra didn't know what to say, other than clearing her throat teasingly. "Well," she grunted in mock haughtiness, "if you must!"

Julie chuckled, not yet realizing the full impact of her words, and went back to work on her counterpoint assignment.

Howard was a serious music student who spent many hours practicing organ, working at the college radio station, programming the classical music segments, or doing intense research in the college library. Julie had never seen him dating any girls—other than the time he spent with her, studying together, going to symphony concerts, and playing piano and organ duets together. They even joined a program team and visited churches in the area to perform in their worship services.

After Bill completed his Medical Specialist Training in the spring of 1966, he came home to Riverdale for a temporary leave. But if he had had any jealous fears about Howard Davidson, they were all dissolved away in Julie's warm hugs and kisses.

"I wish you didn't have to go back," she said over and over.

"I know, baby," he whispered, always caressing her face and kissing her neck. "But you know why I had to leave home. I just wish it didn't mean leaving you, too."

Julie well knew all the reasons, and she understood perfectly, though she didn't like it. *Can our love possibly survive another year and a half of living apart? We are not teeny boppers anymore. I love Bill so* much. *I will wait for him for an eternity if I have to!*

Chapter 14. Sandra Gets Married

Sandra smiled to herself as she opened her bedroom curtains to let in the June morning sun. Too excited to eat, Sandra showered and dressed and waited. Then an old scrapbook in the corner of her closet caught her eye. She sat down and thumbed through it. There were pictures of high school and very familiar faces. The snapshots were candid shots Julie had taken, and now Sandra laughed out loud at the memorable scenes.

Julie had grown up very much since high school days. She had known the childhood agony of young and foolish first "love" with Allen Macintosh, the excitement of dating "older man" Bob Miller the summer of '62, and then the magic April night on Rainbow Pier when Bill Johnson had come into her life.

"Sandra, honey, are you ready yet?" The voice broke through her thoughts.

"Yes, Daddy," she called. "I'll be right there."

Sandra smiled inside as she walked out to the car with her new family. It had been so hard for so long after Mommie had died, but Sandra and her father shared a strong faith in God. Now he was happy with the new Mrs. Lee.

She could hardly believe the years had finally passed, that she and Bob had finally graduated together from La Paloma College and were ready to begin their teaching careers. Graduation had been wonderful but was definitely overshadowed by the momentous event now about to take place.

While Sandra waited for Julie to arrive in the bridal room at the church, her mind wandered again. Riverdale, like the people who lived in it, had changed, too. The "little kids" who once had been so unimportant to Riverdale were now the center of everything, and the "big kids" had all grown up and many of them had moved away.

At that moment, Julie appeared, duly excited. "Well, Sandra, it's almost time for the big moment!"

Sandra smiled. Then she sighed. "Oh, Julie, just think. In just a few minutes, Bob will stand up there on the platform just waiting for his bride!"

"Oh, Sandra! How could things be any more perfect? You know, when I first met Allen at Highview, I was so childish and stupid. I am *so* glad he broke up with me that weekend at Beach City and that Bill was there. Sandra, I love Bill so much! And I never dreamed that I would meet my best friend and soulmate Howard Davidson at La Paloma College. God has been so good to us both. Sandra, we're the two luckiest girls in the entire world!"

"Julie, our cue's coming pretty quick," Sandra whispered. "This is it!"

It was just a few seconds until the *Bridal Processional* began, but in that few seconds Sandra's life seemed to pass through her mind. She remembered the Christmases that she and Bob had spent with Bill and Julie and all the plans they had made for the coming years. Of course, their courtship and engagement had been long. She had even had a brief fling with Kurt Gaston, but that was all forgotten now.

Sandra and Julie were grownup women, not little girls of Riverdale any more. The *Bridal Chorus* had begun, and Julie as maid of honor had started down the aisle, her eyes transfixed on Bill, who stood behind Bob as his best man. Her heart skipped a beat, as it always did when she looked at him, and her heart seemed to melt into a hot puddle right inside her chest. She knew how difficult it had been for him to get leave time from the Army to come home to Riverdale for Sandra and Bob's wedding. But it was so important to Julie for him to be there. He would not disappoint her if there was any way to avoid it.

A little nervously, Sandra smiled at her father and took his arm. Then they started down the aisle toward the minister on the platform where Bob stood—waiting for his bride.

But Bill and Julie were in a world of their own, gazing at each other from opposite sides of the platform, past Bob and Sandra, past this time of separation with Julie at college and Bill stationed far away on an Army base. Julie thought she had never seen Bill look so handsome, as he stood straight and tall in his rented tux. She could almost imagine what he might look like as a groom!

Unknown to Julie through Bill's loving gaze at her, he was admiring the blue satin brocade maid of honor dress she was wearing and imagining what *she* would look like in white lace and pearls and a long, white veil trailing down behind her....

Chapter 15. Bill Proposes to Julie

Soon the ceremony was over and all the wedding guests crowded into the new fellowship hall that the church had built when Sandra and Julie had been away at college. Bill and Julie were caught up in the festivities as they watched Bob and Sandra cut their wedding cake, feed each other a bite, then wash it down with the Hawaiian punch. There were presents to open, and then Bob threw a garter from Sandra's knee. From somewhere back in the crowd, a familiar form rushed forward, and Julie watched Allen Macintosh catch Sandra's garter that Bob tossed behind him. At last, it was time for Sandra to throw her bouquet.

Julie stood in the line of excited, giggling bridesmaids, never really expecting to catch Sandra's bouquet. As the flowery bundle soared high above the crowd, Julie thought she felt very familiar hands on her waist, urging her forward just a little. She didn't have time to turn to see that it was Bill behind her as she lunged forward—and caught Sandra's bouquet! There were cheers and laughs and teases, but Julie clutched the flowers tightly as if they might disappear.

Bill chuckled, and as usual, could not resist kissing her left ear. Julie turned, looking up into his face. The crowd's attention dispersed, and Bob and Sandra disappeared to change clothes before Bill and Julie would drive them—in Bill's '57 Chevy—to an undisclosed destination.

Julie and Bill soon found themselves in the back doorway of the fellowship hall, staring up into the June night sky. Bill put his arms around Julie and turned her to face him, planting a kiss on her forehead, and then another on her lips. He lifted her hands—still holding the bouquet—into his.

"I love you, Kitten," he said affectionately. Then he winked. "I knew you would catch that bouquet!"

"Oh, really, now?" She raised an eyebrow.

He nodded, gazing into her questioning eyes, unable to hide his grin. Then he hugged her just a little tighter as he reached one hand into his pants pocket. And then he kneeled in front of Julie.

"Julie Scott," he began, "will you marry me?" He held up the ring that had been in his pants pocket.

"Oh, yes, Bill Johnson!" she laughed as she let him put the ring on her finger. "Oh, yes! That would be absolutely... marvelous!"

Chapter 16. Bill Goes to Vietnam

When the next school year began—the year that would end with Julie's college graduation—Sandra and Bob had accepted their first teaching assignment and had moved to Simi Valley. This was the first year that Julie had lived alone in the dorm. At first she didn't like it, but she quickly got used to the quiet solitude that allowed her the time and space she needed to focus on her senior year studies.

After a summer concert tour, during which he performed at Carnegie Hall, Howard Davidson was back at La Paloma for his senior year. It took him three weeks, though, to notice Julie's engagement ring.

"It's your boyfriend, Bill Johnson, I presume," he began.

"Why, yes, of course," she replied. "Who else *would* it be?"

"Well, it could have been me," he said, shocking her.

Julie laughed curiously. "Oh, really, now?"

"I was really hoping you could go on tour with me next summer," Howard continued. "I really could have used a good page turner this past summer. Anyway, you could do piano solos during my intermissions. Julie," he looked deeply into her eyes now, taking her fingers into his hands, "you *are* that good!"

She blushed but did not pull her hands away from him. "I don't know, Howard. I've got a wedding to plan."

"But that's an entire year away, isn't it? Not until next fall."

"Next November, when Bill is due for discharge from the Army."

"Think about it," he urged. "Seriously!"

Julie and Howard continued their friendship, including study and practice sessions, concert attendance, and their own performance engagements. Julie said nothing more about her engagement to Bill, but now and then she caught Howard looking at her ring.

Then came the dreaded phone call from Bill.

"I don't think we should be engaged for a while," he said blatantly.

Julie was stunned and speechless! Only the sudden stab of pain that she felt exceeded her shock. *What was going wrong? Had Bill met someone else? Maybe it was that cute young female recruit that followed him around every time they went on town leave in Tacoma, Washington.* Julie started to cry.

"Oh, baby, baby! Please don't cry!" Bill begged, hearing her sobs. "I love you so much!"

"Then what's wrong? What is it, darling?" she pleaded.

Bill was silent for a very long time before he spoke. "My unit is being shipped out to Vietnam next Tuesday."

At once Julie was relieved and frightened—relieved that he still loved her, but very frightened that he was going to Vietnam—what they had both feared for many months.

"I will not make you wait for me when my life will be in danger," he told her. "I may not come home alive, baby! I am an Infantry Medic, you know. I will be where the fighting is very intense, honey. I have to go through this, but you do not. I will not allow you to be in that situation because I love you too much for that. So I must set you free, my love."

"Oh, Bill!" she whispered through her tears. "I would die if I ever lost you!"

He sighed. "I know, Kitten. This is a terrible war. If I had a choice—"

"Do you want the ring back?" she ventured.

"No, darling, it's yours," he answered quickly.

"Then do you want me not to wear it?" she asked.

"That's up to you, baby," he said sadly. "But I know I cannot hold you to our promises of marriage until I return safely to the United States."

Julie could not hide her sadness from Howard when they were together. Howard tried to encourage her to have positive thoughts, but mostly about herself, her senior piano recital planned for next spring, and their graduation and career plans. Howard had become very anti-war, anti-military, and anti-Vietnam. He even had connections to a secret underground group that helped young men get to Canada to avoid being drafted. Knowing this did not help Julie's frame of mind, but she said nothing to Howard about her distress over this.

There were a few times Julie was nearly tempted to take off the ring. But she didn't want to have to answer questions, especially from Howard. She often watched other girls with their boyfriends, and it only made her that much more "homesick" for Bill. Then she started *really* observing guys and usually ended up wondering how the girls could even stand boys! "Yuck!" was her frequent conclusion, followed by, "I'm *so* glad Bill isn't like that!"

Of course, Howard wasn't "like that," either. Howard, who by now truly was Julie's best friend and soulmate, felt so comfortable to be with, as they shared their personal and professional goals and dreams with each other.

Christmas came and went, a rather bleak interlude in Julie's life without Bill. Hardly a day went by that Julie didn't shed a tear or two—and sometimes many tears—especially when Bill's letters were delayed. And when the letters did arrive, Bill often filled them with hair-raising accounts of his terrifying experiences on the front lines as an Infantry Medic. Surely he would have nightmares of those horrendous times for years to come! *Would these months of horror change her sweet loving Bill into something cold and hard? She prayed they would not, but she knew that in reality war changes people!*

When Julie returned to the dorm after Christmas vacation, it surprised her to see a thin young woman standing in front of her door, alternately looking at some papers in her hand and peering at Julie's door, then up and down the empty hallway. Upon seeing Julie, she broke into a dimpled grin. "Are you Julie Scott?" she asked, not at all shy.

"Yes," answered Julie. "Who are you?"

The other girl tilted her head rather sheepishly. "I'm really sorry for all this," she began. "Apparently a *lot* of second-semester freshmen have enrolled, and the freshman dorm is *way* overcrowded. They've even put a bunch of girls three to a room! Anyway, Dean Cushman moved several of us over here, and I guess the girls without roommates here were the first ones they picked."

"Huh?" Julie asked, confused. "Picked for what?"

"Oh!" The newcomer extended her hand boldly toward Julie. "Hi, I'm your new roommate. My name is Janelle Radclyffe."

Chapter 17. Julie's Senior Year at College

Once again Julie's dorm room was buzzing with activity and conversation, much as it had been when she had roomed with Sandra Lee, now Sandra Miller. Janelle, while an elementary education major like Sandra, was vastly different. She was wiry and energetic, with a nonstop smile and nearly nonstop chatter which entertained Julie—unless she was trying to complete a Counterpoint II assignment.

Janelle was outgoing and outspoken and became very animated in discussions involving controversial topics in any arena. Like Julie, she was a brilliant scholar. Julie, quiet and demure, enjoyed both the challenge of Janelle's intellect and the camaraderie of her companionship. Julie felt an undeniable bond with Janelle, almost as if they had been sisters and best friends since they were little girls.

Unlike Sandra, Janelle really didn't like boys very well even though she had three brothers. And Julie could understand much of Janelle's rationale as she freely shared her many observations about male members of the species.

"What gives *them* the right to think they can control us?" Janelle would often ask rhetorically. "They treat women like possessions or property, not like persons," she would say.

Julie agreed with Janelle's assessment of men and boys, but she would usually end up saying, "But Bill's not like most guys!" or "Howard's not like that." And Janelle would have to agree, at least about Howard, with whom she soon became acquainted through Julie. As for Bill, she could only take Julie's word for it.

Julie played her senior piano recital early in the spring, and it was an overwhelming success. She played representative works of Bach, Beethoven, Brahms, and her favorite, Chopin. She was very surprised that Howard and Janelle had jointly planned, designed, and ordered a beautiful cake for her reception, along with matching cocktail napkins.

After all the guests had left the reception, Janelle could tell that Howard wanted to talk to Julie—alone. She excused herself by saying she would take the leftover cake back to the dorm.

In the empty auditorium, Howard and Julie sat side by side on the darkened stage on the piano bench, leaning back against the now-silent keyboard. Howard put his arm around Julie, surprising her somewhat.

"I wanted you to be the first to know, Julie," he began. "I've had a job offer for next school year."

"Howard, that's wonderful! What and where?" Julie was truly delighted for him.

"It's an exclusive little private boarding school in North Carolina—"

"North Carolina!" Julie wrinkled her nose and began imitating a thick Southern accent as she said, "Why on earth would y'all want to go *there?*"

Howard laughed at Julie's ridiculous twang. "It's not so bad! They tell me there's a great music department with lots of interest in keyboard, and they need a superb organ and piano teacher. Apparently they heard about me from my tours last summer."

"Well," Julie said, "are you going to take it?"

"I think so," said Howard, "but—" He stopped.

"But what?"

"They also need an excellent piano teacher for the overflow students—and a dean for the girls' dormitory."

Julie looked at him, startled, realizing what he had just said. "Oh, no!" she laughed, "not me! I will *not* be a girls' dean!"

"Oh, it couldn't be all that hard—just babysitting a bunch of girls—could it? Anyway, I'd love to have you in the music department with me. There are *so* many possibilities, projects we could accomplish together."

"I don't know, Howard. I don't know what Bill's going to want to do when he gets home from Vietnam, where he'll want to live, or even when we'll get married."

"Well, couldn't he go to North Carolina as easily as California? I mean, if he wanted to."

Julie was silent. "I'll think about it."

Howard suddenly gave Julie a little squeeze, surprising her even more. But she said nothing.

As they walked back to the girls' dorm, she felt Howard take her hand. "Julie," he said, "you are my very best friend. I—I just want to work with you in our first jobs after graduation. You are *so* talented and smart. After these past two years of studying and performing together—well, I just don't want to lose that!"

Julie knew it was true, the way she and Howard played duets in perfect synchronization with each other. It was almost as if they could read each other's minds. Still, if Howard felt this strongly about her, about a future with her, why had it never occurred to him to become romantic, even though he had teased about marriage to her just so they could keep playing duets together? Not that she would have wanted that complication in her life! But it made her wonder....

It was Dean Cushman who called Julie into her office less than a week later with a letter she handed to Julie. "This came today from Orchill Hills Academy in North Carolina," the older woman began. "They need a girls' dean and a piano teacher."

Julie opened her mouth, but no sound came out. *Howard has not had time to contact them, and I haven't given him a definite answer, anyway! He already gave them my name before he even talked to me!*

"You are very well qualified, Julie," Dean Cushman continued. "I have your cumulative folder here." She leafed through the top sheets. "Have you ever considered being a girls' dean?"

Julie shook her head.

Dean Cushman smiled and spent the next hour and a half telling Julie about the job of being a dormitory dean. Near the end, she lowered her voice slightly as she said, "There *is* one thing you need to be very much on the alert for. Sometimes there are... things... that happen in girls' dorms—things... between girls. You've got to recognize the signs and put a quick end to... those things."

Julie really didn't know what to say. She just nodded and smiled. But she took the letter from Orchill Hills and the photos of the campus it contained. She was quite impressed with the school itself and was totally breathless at seeing the beautiful scenery of the North Carolina country. "God's country," Dean Cushman had said, so very different from the dry hills of Riverdale Valley. It would be an adventure!

That night Julie sat down and wrote a long letter to Bill. The next day she got a letter from Bill, one that he had written and mailed long before she had mailed hers. Despite his resolve to not hold her to any promises of marriage before he returned home, he talked more and more about what their life together might be like.

"I want four children," was one of his frequent comments. They had never even talked about children when they had been together! Other than how to keep from having babies right then! Now Julie realized that having four babies—two boys and two girls—had always been her dream, too! And to have Bill's children! She could think of nothing she would love better. *But what about her piano teaching career?* She decided she would call Sandra in Simi Valley.

"What's saying you can't have both?" her childhood friend said. "You could teach at Orchill Hills a couple of years, then after you and Bill have kids, you could teach piano lessons at home, maybe even keep your Orchill Hills students if you lived close enough to the Academy."

Julie thought that made sense. She loved Bill so much and didn't want to lose him! Yet, how could she possibly pass up this opportunity to teach at such a prestigious place as Orchill Hills? She wrote another letter to Bill.

It surprised her to receive a reply from Bill so soon. "I have never thought about living anywhere else besides California, Kitten," he wrote back. "I was born in Los Angeles, and now that Mom has moved to Riverdale and your Momma lives there, too, how could we possibly live in North Carolina!"

But, like Julie, Bill wrote another letter the very next day. "You won't believe this," he began, "but I got a letter today from my oldest brother Tom. You probably didn't know that he moved to North Carolina a few years ago when he married Molly White, who has a daughter named Annie. He's a doctor there, and he says that it's a great place to live and raise a family."

Julie's heart skipped a beat, as she sighed contentedly, looked longingly and lovingly at Bill's senior picture on her dresser. She clutched the precious ring Bill had given her very close to her heart.

Chapter 18. Julie and Howard Graduate

Graduation ceremonies for Julie and Howard were very festive, especially as the two lifelong best friends shared the excitement of beginning their teaching careers together at Orchill Hills Academy. They would leave for North Carolina early in July to get settled in, to get the music building organized and ready for students, and—for Julie—to get oriented to the job of being the girls' dean. On the way, Howard and Julie had a mini-itinerary of concert performances scheduled in Phoenix, Denver, Chicago, and Washington, D.C. Finally, they would both attend the annual teachers' convention in Miami before starting the school year.

Howard helped Julie move out of her dorm room. Janelle would stay at La Paloma for the summer.

"Oh, by the way," Julie told them both, "did you hear that Allen Macintosh is getting married next week?"

Howard chuckled, remembering how Allen had caught the garter at Sandra and Bob's wedding. Howard knew, too, of all the meanness that Allen had heaped upon Julie when he was her boyfriend during those long-ago high school years.

"Yeah, I heard," Janelle interjected. "Some nurse named Shirley, isn't it?"

"I think so," Julie said. "Someone said she's very 'wholesome.'"

Howard laughed, giving Julie a sisterly hug. "Well, that's *his* loss!" Howard said with a tone of disdain.

Janelle rolled her eyes.

As Howard made one last trip to Julie's car with her last box, Julie turned to say goodbye to Janelle and found her staring out their third-story window. Julie put her arm around Janelle.

"You've been such a great roommate," Julie said. "I'll miss you."

When Janelle turned to face Julie, there were tears in her eyes—the first time Julie had seen tears in Janelle's normally sparkling countenance. Her voice was low and cracked with emotion. "I'll miss you more than you know," she said. Then, impulsively, Janelle threw her arms around Julie and hugged her full body for a timeless moment.

Julie relaxed into her embrace. "You'll write to me in North Carolina, won't you?"

"I will *never* lose touch with you," Janelle promised.

On Fourth of July weekend, Julie was at home in Riverdale, still trying to convince Momma that she was "grown up enough" to move across country and live on her own. Howard stayed at Julie's house in a spare bedroom, and then they would drive across the country to North Carolina together, pulling a small U-Haul trailer with their belongings, and doing their concert tour.

Howard was playing the piano when Julie came in with the mail.

"This is odd," she said, holding up a letter. "It's an envelope from Orchill Hills, but it looks like a personal letter." She tore it open and began to read. "Hmm," she said, more to herself than to Howard, "it's from someone named Linda Niles, a sophomore girl. She says they have assigned her to be my 'student hostess' or something like that, since she's a dorm monitor and I'm the new dean. I guess it's a kind of welcome letter or something."

"Oh, yes," Howard said, remembering that he had forgotten to tell Julie about the letter he had received. "I got a similar letter from the girl who will be my student secretary in the Music Department. I had already heard about her from the band teacher, though, as she is a very brilliant student and talented soprano. She's really operatic quality."

"Wow, that's something!" Julie smiled. "At least we'll already know two of the students when we get there. What's her name?"

Howard pulled an envelope from the Bach Three-Part Inventions he had been practicing and unfolded the letter. "Let's see here," he said, scanning it. "Oh, yes, it's Lina Jackson."

That was when Bill showed up unexpectedly. The Army had granted him, at the last minute, a week's "R&R" from Vietnam to Hawaii, but he scheduled a flight to Riverdale instead. No one knew until he called his mother from the L.A. airport. He was under strict orders not to enter the continental United States while on R&R.

He would be AWOL, a court martial offense, if he did! But he had to come home, anyway. He had to see Julie! He had sensed there was a growing bond between Julie and Howard, one that he felt Julie did not even know existed. That bond was the music that they both shared a deep and abiding passion for. *What if...?*

But soon his '57 Chevy appeared in Julie's driveway.

"Bill!" Julie screamed in delight when she answered the door, rushing into his outstretched arms. She cried tears of joy. "How—why—what are you doing here!" And he told her the story.

Howard sauntered out into the living room, surprised to see Bill. Bill saw Howard, whom he had first met last summer at Sandra and Bob's wedding. An instant surge of jealousy swept through him, even though his mind—or at least Julie's letters—told him that there was nothing more than friendship between Howard and Julie. The two young men exchanged pleasantries, then there was an awkward silence, until Howard decided he really needed to get back to his practicing. Bill had seen that unmistakable look on Howard's face, with feelings plainly written there just as if by ink. Bill and Julie went out to the porch swing to talk.

Bill did not speak for a long time. He put his arm around Julie and held her close. Finally he said, "Howard really likes you, Kitten."

She nodded. "He's been my best friend on campus these past two years. Well, he and Janelle this past semester. They've both been great to me."

"I know, sweetheart," he agreed, "and I'm glad they've been there for you since I haven't been here."

Julie hugged Bill close. "Oh, baby, I have missed you *so* much! I can hardly wait for the next four months to pass when you'll be home for good!"

"A lot can happen in four months, baby," he spoke pensively. "There's still no guarantee I'll return home."

A shiver of fear shot through Julie, as it always did when she thought of anything ever happening to Bill. "You *will!*" she exclaimed. "Don't even *think* of anything else!"

"I want to come home alive," he said. "More than anything else I want to come home to you and spend the rest of my life with you. But—" He paused. "My guess is that Howard would like to do that very much, too."

"Howard is my best friend—that's all!" she insisted. "I love him like a brother. But you—Bill, you are the love of my life, my ultimate Prince Charming! Forever and always!" She reached up, putting her arms around his neck, and he pulled her onto his lap. They kissed, gently and sweetly at first, then with increasing passion and desire.

After a while, Bill lifted her gently from his lap and stood up, still embracing her. Then he took her hand, and they walked to his car. She did not have to ask where they were going now. Bill's '57 Chevy made its way in the growing twilight up to the Riverdale Bowl, across the parking lot, and onto the dirt road that led to the hay pits.

It was a balmy summer night, and it seemed like a million stars shone in the velvet-black night sky. Soon the Riverdale fireworks would begin, but Julie and Bill had other thoughts on their minds.

"I have to go back tomorrow," he said, once they settled into the hay pit on the blanket that Bill always kept in his car.

She sighed. "And day after tomorrow Howard and I will need to drive to Orchill Hills."

He squeezed her. "I will never share you, my love. I will fight to fill any desire that you have to the fullest extent that I can—and three times over. I will make every dream and fantasy come true for you!"

A feeling of hot electricity surged through Julie's entire mind and body at Bill's words. *Truly, to love and to be loved is the greatest joy on earth!*

Making love was inevitable. It had been so long! Their every embrace and caress was slow and gentle and bonding. The minutes turned into hours, until the fireworks, clearly seen in the skies over Riverdale, had come and gone. But Julie and Bill knew only the fireworks that were exploding, over and over, inside both of them. They both knew that, despite a still uncertain future, their love was for eternity. No matter what.

As they finally lay together in deep contentment before they knew they would have to leave their special place, Bill held her very close. His voice broke the cozy silence. "What are you thinking, my love?" he asked, lazily tracing her lips with his finger.

She grinned, then kissed his hand, as she looked up into his intense blue eyes, like pools of pure love, and windows to his very soul. "Marvelous, baby!" she said, as she always did. "Just marvelous!"

Chapter 19. How Did It Really End?

L et's ask each of the key players in this fantasy...

JULIE JOHNSON

Well, this should not be too hard to figure out, should it?!? Of course, Bill came home safely to me four months after his illegal R&R. He came to North Carolina where Howard and I were teaching at Orchill Hills Academy. We had a beautiful Christmas wedding with Howard playing the organ, then Bill and I moved off campus while I continued to teach piano at Orchill Hills. He worked in town for a few years until we could save up enough money to move back to Riverdale where we still live. Our four children are beautiful and brilliant. Our daughters are teachers and artists, and our sons are computer geniuses and astute business executives. Most of all, the intense love that we have shared since 1963 is for eternity!

ANNIE JOHNSON

One day I walked into my mom's house and saw a picture of Bill Johnson, my stepdad's youngest brother. I said, "That is the man I'm going to marry and spend the rest of my life with." And I did. I began writing to Bill while he was still in Vietnam, even though he was engaged to Julie who worked in North Carolina. When he came home, he went to North Carolina, but came to his brother's house first, and met my mom and me. That was all it took! We fell in love at first sight, and the rest is history. Bill and I got married, moved back to California, and became friends with Bob and Sandra Miller. Bill never even mentioned Julie again until recently when he found out she's now a lesbian! Sorry, Bill, you've got the wrong body parts for her.

HOWARD DAVIDSON

Julie and I began our teaching careers in North Carolina. Even though Julie thought she was going to marry Bill Johnson when he came home from the Army, she was so focused on her work as girls' dean and piano teacher that she kept postponing her wedding. After a while, Bill gave up on her and married a local girl. I was ecstatic to have Julie all to myself! We got married and seven years later we discovered I was gay and she was a lesbian. We remained legally married, however, and bought a big elegant house in San Francisco. Although I have had many gay lovers over the years, my Orchill Hills student secretary, Lina Jackson, came to live with us and became Julie's lover. They were each artificially inseminated with my superior donor sperm. Lina and Julie each had one child, both of them intelligent, musical, and superior in every way.

JANELLE RADCLYFFE

I never forgot my roommate Julie Scott! She was sweet and shy, sensitive and intelligent, and lots of fun to be with. After she left La Paloma, I finished college and began my teaching career. I fell in love with Caitlin, and we lived together for a few years until she broke my heart and got married to a man. But I always stayed in touch with Julie. When her marriage broke up, I invited her to come stay with me for a while. She had two babies by that time and did not want to live on welfare. We quickly fell in love! She stayed at home and taught piano while I continued to teach school. Julie and I raised her children together and became active in supporting gay rights. She became a bold and assertive feminist woman, and I became an understanding and gentle stepmother. We are proud of our independent children who moved out and have lived on their own from a very early age.

ALLEN MACINTOSH

Yes, I remember Julie Scott. I liked her because of her intelligence and devotion to me. It was easy to make her laugh, make her cry, and get her to do just about anything I wanted her to. All I had to do was tell her I loved her, and she always believed me, no matter how badly I treated her. But breaking up with her was the biggest mistake of my life. Although I was married for many years to Shirley, a sensible woman who achieved a brilliant career and was a model wife and mother, after our divorce I contacted Julie again. But by then it was too late for me. Julie had definitely moved on with her life and, while cordial to me, no longer had any romantic interest in me. I told her to "bloom where you're planted." I don't know why I said that.

LINA REITER

My name was Lina Jackson at Orchill Hills Academy where I first met Howard Davidson and Julie Scott. I so loved their music! I never forgot them, even after they left North Carolina. Julie and I, each in our separate worlds, got married, had babies, and raised them halfway to adulthood before our respective marriages fell apart. I moved across the country to begin my new life in California as a business partner with Howard at *Davidson Music Press*, and I found Julie on the internet! We discovered how much we had in common, what with our mothering, our musical interests, and most of all our mutual love for Howard Davidson and his music. We lived together and finished raising our children together. The children have all become responsible, productive young adults. Now in midlife, Julie and I both have brilliant careers as professional musicians and web designers, and plan to spend our golden years in luxury.

BILL JOHNSON

Hey, no one has asked me what really happened in Riverdale! Yes, I knew Julie Scott. I fell in love with Julie that night in Beach City when we walked hand in hand on Rainbow Pier. We played in the Riverdale hay pits, where I kissed her and made love to her for the very first time. We were engaged to be married until I visited my older brother in North Carolina and met my sister-in-law's beautiful daughter, Annie. We have been married for many decades, have children and grandchildren, and I have had a stable career in computers with the same company for all these years. I'm very much in love with the woman I was always meant to marry, who is beautiful and brilliant and sexy. Our love is forever and always!

JULIANA HARVARD

Who is this Julie Scott person, anyway? And how does she presume to use my name to copyright her lousy stories? Her writing is so arcane. She must have been a very confused and dysfunctional teenager, especially to have written such melodramatic trash about her life! As for me, I'm the legendary "Suburban Married Lady" who is writing a series of brilliant autobiographical novels about my life—my marriages, my children, my divorces, my coming out as a bisexual woman, my passionate love affairs with persons of both genders and orientations, and my current fascinating career in Silicon Valley as a high-tech service engineer and successful author. Do I sound like that pitiful Julie Scott of long-ago Riverdale?!?

Afterword

Juliana Harvard is working on her epic autobiographical novel, *Suburban Married Lady*, which follows after the last book in the *It Happened in Riverdale* series, *More Riverdale Stories*. Keep up to date with Ms. Harvard's works at *Lady J's Place*[1] or *Juliana Harvard, Author*[2] on Facebook. Some of her stories are also available on *Inkitt*[3]

---

1. *https://lemi-hegarty.website/ladyj/*

2. *https://www.facebook.com/JulianaScottHarvard/*

3. *https://www.inkitt.com/julianascottharvard*

Don't miss out!

Visit the website below and you can sign up to receive emails whenever Juliana Harvard publishes a new book. There's no charge and no obligation.

https://books2read.com/r/B-A-EPQM-GRAOB

BOOKS 2 READ

Connecting independent readers to independent writers.

Also by Juliana Harvard

About the Author

Juliana Harvard's writing spans more than five decades, from her adolescence until well past midlife. It is reflective of her most emotional moments, sometimes of ecstasy and wonder, sometimes of sadness and pain, and other times of sweet melancholy and contentment beyond words.

DISCLAIMER: "These are works of fiction. Any similarities to persons and places are frequent, intentional, and occasionally brazen, but generally fragmentary, inconsistent, and disguised with fanciful invention."

–Stephen Minot, *Three Genres*